PEDRO'S
MYSTERY
CLUB

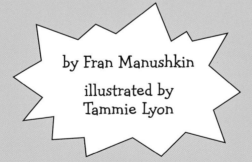

by Fran Manushkin

illustrated by
Tammie Lyon

PICTURE WINDOW BOOKS
a capstone imprint

Pedro is published by Picture Window Books,
a Capstone Imprint
1710 Roe Crest Drive
North Mankato, Minnesota 56003
www.mycapstone.com

Text © 2017 Fran Manushkin
Illustrations © 2017 Picture Window Books

Library of Congress Cataloging-in-Publication Data
Names: Manushkin, Fran, author. | Lyon, Tammie, illustrator.
Title: Pedro's mystery club / by Fran Manushkin ; illustrator, Tammie Lyon.
Description: North Mankato, Minnesota : Picture Window Books, a Capstone
    imprint, 2016. | ?2017 | Series: Pedro | Summary: Pedro forms a new club
    with his friends dedicated to solving mysteries--and the first two
    assignments are finding his mother's locket, and his father's cell phone.
Identifiers: LCCN 2015046885| ISBN 9781515800842 (library binding) | ISBN
    9781515800880 (pbk.) | ISBN 9781515800927 (ebook (pdf))
Subjects: LCSH: Hispanic Americans—Juvenile fiction. | Lost articles—Juvenile
    fiction. | Clubs—Juvenile fiction. | Friendship—Juvenile fiction. | CYAC: Mystery
    and detective stories. | Hispanic Americans—Fiction. | Lost and found
    possessions—Fiction. | Clubs—Fiction. | Friendship—Fiction.
Classification: LCC PZ7.M3195 Pco 2016 | DDC 813.54—dc23
LC record available at http://lccn.loc.gov/2015046885

Designer: Aruna Rangarajan and Tracy McCabe
Design Elements: Shutterstock

Photo Credits:
Greg Holch, pg. 26
Tammie Lyon, pg. 26

Table of Contents

Chapter 1
A Small Mystery

"I am starting a mystery club!" Pedro told Katie and JoJo. "We can have our meetings here in my new tree house."

"Cool idea!" said JoJo.

"I'm great at solving

mysteries," said Katie Woo.

"I always know where Mom

hides my birthday presents."

"I have a mystery for you," said Pedro's mom. "I can't find my locket."

"That is a small mystery," said Pedro. "But it's a good start."

Pedro wrote down the clues.

"Where did you go today?" he

asked his mom.

"I went to the store to get

chocolate-chip cookie mix,"

she said.

"I know what to do," said Pedro. "We will follow the path you took and find your locket. It will be hard work. So when we come back, we will need those cookies."

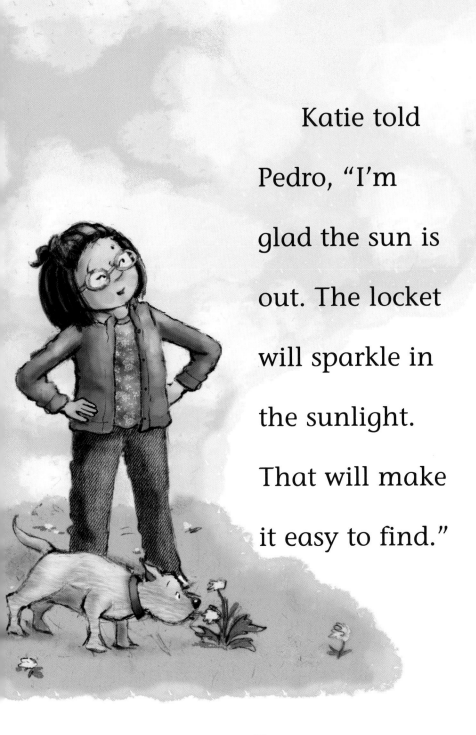

Katie told Pedro, "I'm glad the sun is out. The locket will sparkle in the sunlight. That will make it easy to find."

"I see it!" yelled Katie. "Oops.

I don't. It's just a dime."

"I found a toy ring," said

JoJo. "It fits my hand."

But they didn't find a locket.

Chapter 2
More Clues

The three friends came to a
big hill. Katie asked, "Do you
think your mom walked up
this hill?"

"No way," said Pedro. "But
I would like to roll down it.
It's fun!"

It was!

"Whoops!" said Pedro. "I lost my notebook."

They climbed back up and found the notebook.

"Solving mysteries is hard work," said Pedro. "I need a drink."

Luckily, his friend Jane was selling lemonade.

"I saw your mom an hour ago," said Jane. "She got a drink on her way to the store."

"Was she wearing her locket?" asked Pedro.

"She wasn't," said Jane. "I always like looking at the photos inside. But she wasn't wearing it."

They rushed home. Pedro told his mom, "Jane didn't see you wearing your locket on the way to the store. It is still here!"

"I have another mystery," said Pedro's dad. "I can't find my new phone!"

"Did you roll down a

hill?" asked Pedro.

"No," said his dad.

They looked for his phone.

They looked for the locket.

No luck.

Chapter 3

Case Closed

Pedro said, "Let's take a break from mystery solving. Let's play soccer!"

Katie kicked the ball. She kicked it too hard, and the ball rolled under a bush.

"I'll get it," yelled Pedro.

As he grabbed the ball, he saw something shiny — his mom's locket!

"Yay, Pedro!" she said. "My locket fell off when I was picking roses."

"Now let's find Dad's phone," said Pedro. "Let's go to our clubhouse. That's a good place to think."

JoJo wondered, "If I were a phone, where would I be?"

Katie said, "I wish that noisy bird would stop chirping. I can't think!"

"That's no bird," said

Pedro. "It's Dad's phone!

Someone is trying to call him."

They followed the sound down

to the grass.

Pedro's dad smiled.

"I dropped it when I was painting your tree house."

Katie Woo smiled too.

"If your family keeps losing things, we will always have mysteries to solve."

"Quick!" said Pedro. "Before that happens, let's have a snack."

The snack was no mystery — it was chocolate chip cookies!

About the Author

Fran Manushkin is the author of many popular picture books, including *Happy in Our Skin*; *Baby, Come Out!*; *Latkes and Applesauce: A Hanukkah Story*; *The Tushy Book*; *The Belly Book*; and *Big Girl Panties*. Fran writes on her beloved Mac computer in New York City, without the help of her two naughty cats, Chaim and Goldy.

About the Illustrator

Tammie Lyon began her love for drawing at a young age while sitting at the kitchen table with her dad. She continued her love of art and eventually attended the Columbus College of Art and Design, where she earned a bachelor's degree in fine art. After a brief career as a professional ballet dancer, she decided to devote herself full-time to illustration. Today she lives with her husband, Lee, in Cincinnati, Ohio. Her dogs, Gus and Dudley, keep her company as she works in her studio.

Glossary

chirping (CHURP-ing)—making a twittering, birdlike sound

clues (KLOOZ)—things that help a person find something or solve a mystery

locket (LOK-it)—a piece of jewelry worn on a chain around the neck, which often contains a photograph

mystery (MISS-tur-ee)—something that has not been explained

shiny (SHY-nee)—bright or glossy-looking

sparkle (SPAR-kuhl)—shine with many flashing points of light

Let's Talk

1. Pedro started a mystery club. If you started your own club, what kind of club would you start? What would you do in your club?

2. Pedro says the clubhouse is a good place to think. What makes it a good place for thinking? Where do you do your best thinking?

3. Have you ever solved a mystery? What happened?

Let's Write

1. Write out the steps Pedro and his friends took to solve the mystery of the lost locket.

2. Pretend the locket is still lost. Make a sign advertising the lost locket. Include a picture and description.

3. Pedro interviewed a witness in this story. Look up the word "witness" and write down the definition. Then write a sentence stating who Pedro's witness is.

JOKE AROUND

🔍 I'm tall when I'm young and I'm short when I'm old. What am I?
a candle

🔍 What has hands but cannot clap?
a clock

🔍 What word becomes shorter if you add two letters to it?
short

🔍 What is at the end of a rainbow?
the letter W

🔍 What gets wetter as it dries?
a towel

🔍 What occurs twice in a week, once in a year, but never in a day?
the letter e

🔍 What has to be broken before you can use it?
an egg

THE FUN DOESN'T STOP HERE!

Discover more at www.capstonekids.com

- 🔍 Videos & Contests
- 🔍 Games & Puzzles
- 🔍 Friends & Favorites
- 🔍 Authors & Illustrators

Find cool websites and more books like this one at www.facthound.com. Just type in the Book ID: 9781515800842 and you're ready to go!